Harry Potter™

MOVIE POSTER BOOK

HEROES

ISBN 978-0-545-23763-5

12 11 10 9 8 7 6 5 4 3 2 1   10 11 12 13 14 15/0
Printed in the U.S.A. First printing, October 2010   40

SCHOLASTIC INC.
NEW YORK TORONTO LONDON AUCKLAND
SYDNEY MEXICO CITY NEW DELHI HONG KONG

HARRY POTTER™

HOUSE:
GRYFFINDOR

PATRONUS:
STAG

FAMILY:
LILY AND JAMES POTTER (PARENTS)

HOBBY/INTEREST:
QUIDDITCH™

EXTRA FACT:
KNOWN AS "THE BOY WHO LIVED"
AND "THE CHOSEN ONE"

HARRY POTTER™

HOUSE:
GRYFFINDOR

PATRONUS:
DOG

FAMILY:
ARTHUR AND MOLLY (PARENTS);
CHARLIE, BILL, PERCY, FRED, GEORGE
AND GINNY WEASLEY (SIBLINGS)

HOBBY/INTEREST:
WIZARD CHESS

EXTRA FACT:
TERRIFIED OF SPIDERS

RON WEASLEY™

RON WEASLEY™

HERMIONE GRANGER™

HOUSE:
GRYFFINDOR

PATRONUS:
OTTER

FAMILY:
MUGGLE-BORN; PARENTS ARE DENTISTS

HOBBY/INTEREST:
READING

EXTRA FACT:
TOP OF HER CLASS

HERMIONE GRANGER™

HOUSE:
GRYFFINDOR

FAMILY:
ALICE AND FRANK LONGBOTTOM (PARENTS)

HOBBY/INTEREST:
HERBOLOGY

EXTRA FACT:
LIVES WITH HIS GRANDMOTHER

NEVILLE LONGBOTTOM™

NEVILLE
LONGBOTTOM

HOUSE:
GRYFFINDOR

FAMILY:
ARTHUR AND MOLLY (PARENTS);
CHARLIE, BILL, PERCY, FRED, GEORGE
AND RON WEASLEY (BROTHERS)

HOBBY/INTEREST:
QUIDDITCH

EXTRA FACT:
POSSESSED BY VOLDEMORT
DURING HER FIRST YEAR AT HOGWARTS

**GINNY
WEASLEY**™

HOUSE:
RAVENCLAW

FAMILY:
XENOPHILIUS LOVEGOOD (FATHER)

PATRONUS:
HARE

EXTRA FACT:
FATHER IS EDITOR OF *THE QUIBBLER*

LUNA LOVEGOOD™

DUMBLEDORE'S ARMY™

PARVATI PATIL

HOUSE:
GRYFFINDOR

LAVENDER BROWN

HOUSE:
GRYFFINDOR

PADMA PATIL

HOUSE:
RAVENCLAW

SEAMUS FINNIGAN

HOUSE:
GRYFFINDOR

COLIN CREEVEY

HOUSE:
GRYFFINDOR

CHO CHANG

HOUSE:
RAVENCLAW

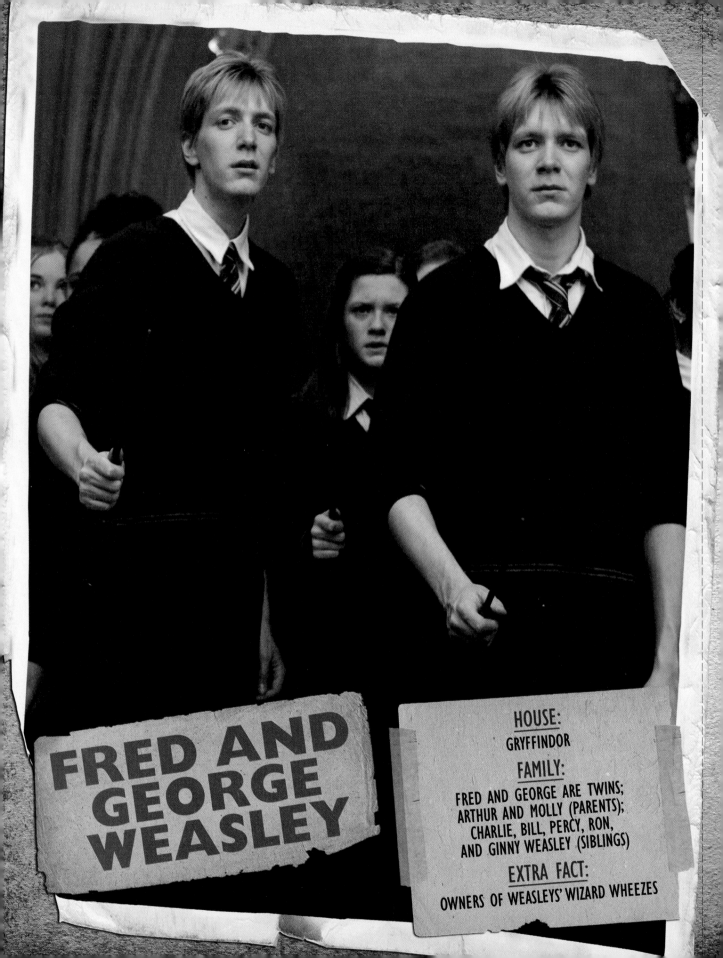

FRED AND GEORGE WEASLEY

HOUSE:
GRYFFINDOR

FAMILY:
FRED AND GEORGE ARE TWINS; ARTHUR AND MOLLY (PARENTS); CHARLIE, BILL, PERCY, RON, AND GINNY WEASLEY (SIBLINGS)

EXTRA FACT:
OWNERS OF WEASLEYS' WIZARD WHEEZES

BILL WEASLEY

HOUSE:
GRYFFINDOR

FAMILY:
ARTHUR AND MOLLY (PARENTS); CHARLIE, BILL, PERCY, RON AND GINNY WEASLEY (SIBLINGS); FLEUR DELACOUR (WIFE)

EXTRA FACT:
BITTEN BY FENRIR GREYBACK

FLEUR DELACOUR WEASLEY

SCHOOL:
BEAUXBATONS

FAMILY:
BILL WEASLEY (HUSBAND); GABRIELLE (SISTER)

EXTRA FACT:
BEAUXBATONS TRIWIZARD CHAMPION DURING HARRY'S FOURTH YEAR AT HOGWARTS

ALBUS DUMBLEDORE™

PATRONUS:
PHOENIX

EXTRA FACTS:
HEADMASTER OF HOGWARTS;
FOUNDER OF THE ORDER OF THE PHOENIX

ALBUS
DUMBLEDORE™

HORACE SLUGHORN

HOUSE:
SLYTHERIN

TEACHES:
POTIONS DURING HARRY'S SIXTH YEAR AT HOGWARTS

FILIUS FLITWICK

HOUSE:
RAVENCLAW

TEACHES:
CHARMS

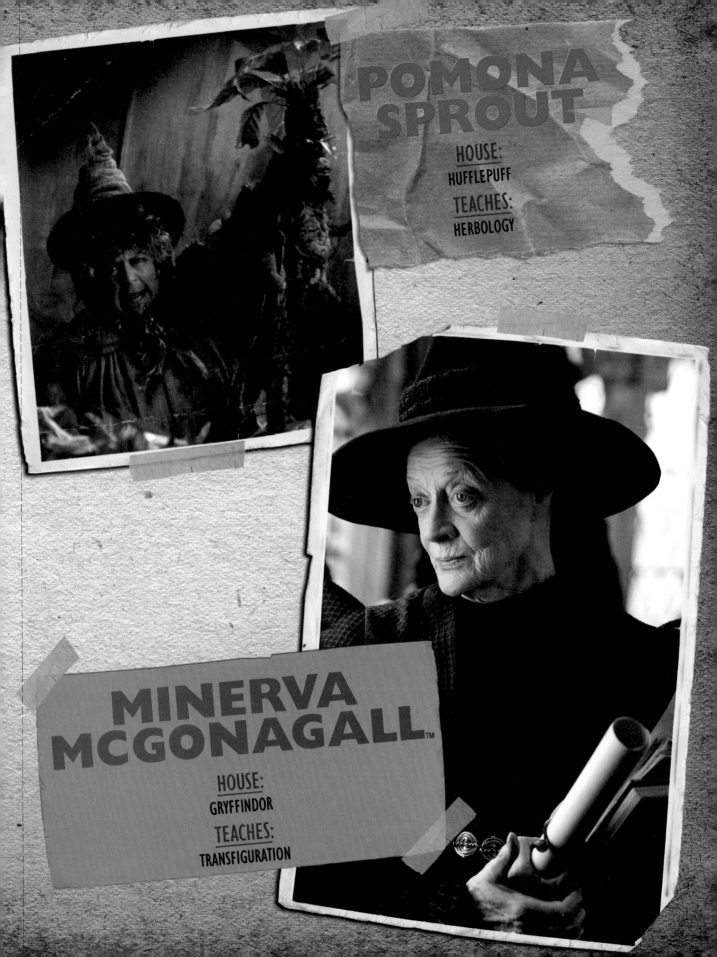

POMONA
SPROUT

HOUSE:
HUFFLEPUFF

TEACHES:
HERBOLOGY

MINERVA
MCGONAGALL™

HOUSE:
GRYFFINDOR

TEACHES:
TRANSFIGURATION

RUBEUS HAGRID™

EXTRA FACTS:

KEEPER OF KEYS AND GROUNDS;
CARE OF MAGICAL CREATURES TEACHER AT HOGWARTS

ABERFORTH
DUMBLEDORE

EXTRA FACTS:
BARMAN AT THE HOG'S HEAD;
ALBUS DUMBLEDORE'S BROTHER

MOLLY WEASLEY

EXTRA FACT:
MEMBER OF THE ORDER OF THE PHOENIX

ARTHUR WEASLEY

<u>EXTRA</u> FACTS:

WORKS IN THE MISUSE OF MUGGLE ARTIFACTS OFFICE IN THE MINISTRY OF MAGIC;
MEMBER OF THE ORDER OF THE PHOENIX

REMUS LUPIN™

EXTRA FACTS:

WEREWOLF; DEFENSE AGAINST THE DARK ARTS TEACHER
DURING HARRY'S THIRD YEAR AT HOGWARTS

NYMPHADORA TONKS™

EXTRA FACTS:
METAMORPHMAGUS; MEMBER OF THE ORDER OF THE PHOENIX

SIRIUS BLACK™

EXTRA FACTS:

ANIMAGUS; MEMBER OF THE ORDER OF THE PHOENIX

ALASTOR "MAD-EYE" MOODY

EXTRA FACTS:
AUROR; MEMBER OF THE ORDER OF THE PHOENIX;
DEFENSE AGAINST THE DARK ARTS TEACHER
DURING HARRY'S FOURTH YEAR AT HOGWARTS;
HAS A MAGICAL EYE AND A WOODEN LEG

ORDER OF THE PHOENIX

CREATED BY ALBUS DUMBLEDORE TO FIGHT LORD VOLDEMORT

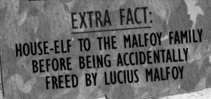

DOBBY™

EXTRA FACT:

HOUSE-ELF TO THE MALFOY FAMILY
BEFORE BEING ACCIDENTALLY
FREED BY LUCIUS MALFOY

KREACHER™

EXTRA FACT:

HOUSE-ELF TO THE BLACK FAMILY
AND LATER TO HARRY POTTER

GRIPHOOK

RACE:

GOBLIN

EXTRA FACT:

GRINGOTTS BANK EMPLOYEE

FAWKES™

DUMBLEDORE'S PHOENIX, FAWKES, PROVIDED THE CORE FEATHER FOR EACH OF HARRY'S AND VOLDEMORT'S WANDS

HEDWIG™

HARRY POTTER'S OWL, HEDWIG, WAS GIVEN TO HIM ON HIS ELEVENTH BIRTHDAY BY RUBEUS HAGRID

CROOKSHANKS™

HERMIONE'S CAT DETECTED SOMETHING ODD ABOUT RON'S RAT SCABBERS DURING THEIR THIRD YEAR AT HOGWARTS

BUCKBEAK™

BUCKBEAK THE HIPPOGRIFF PLAYED A CRUCIAL ROLE IN GETTING SIRIUS BLACK TO SAFETY DURING HARRY'S THIRD YEAR AT HOGWARTS

SEVERUS SNAPE™

PATRONUS:
DOE

EXTRA FACTS:
POTIONS MASTER DURING HARRY'S FIRST FIVE YEARS AT HOGWARTS;
DEFENSE AGAINST THE DARK ARTS TEACHER DURING HARRY'S SIXTH YEAR AT HOGWARTS;
HEADMASTER OF HOGWARTS AFTER HARRY LEAVES SCHOOL